21st Century's Rizal and Rivera

Densei

Ukiyoto Publishing

All global publishing rights are held by

Ukiyoto Publishing

Published in 2024

Content Copyright © Densei

ISBN 9789361720802s

*All rights reserved.
No part of this publication may be reproduced,
transmitted, or stored in a retrieval system, in any
form by any means, electronic, mechanical,
photocopying, recording or otherwise, without the
prior permission of the publisher.*

The moral rights of the authors have been asserted.

*This is a work of fiction. Names, characters, businesses,
places, events, locales, and incidents are either the
products of the author's imagination or used in a
fictitious manner. Any resemblance to actual persons,
living or dead, or actual events is purely coincidental.*

*This book is sold subject to the condition that it shall
not by way of trade or otherwise, be lent, resold, hired
out or otherwise circulated, without the publisher's
prior consent, in any form of binding or cover other
than that in which it is published.*

www.ukiyoto.com

Acknowledgement

To my family who does not have any idea about this, I hope you will not know anything about this at all. And to my sweetest friends; Rein, Yna, Cams, Marian, and Zhas, I am forever indebted to you for your continual support to whatever I do in my life. I love you all with all my heart.

I hereby dedicate this book to everyone with unsent letters. And to you, because I will not be able to start this book without you.

Contents

This empty canvas that they misunderstood, I wanna paint you in it but I'm not good.   1

Why can't we for once say what we want, say what we feel.   8

Call in the morning, say that you love me, I'm always waiting, I'm always waiting.   11

Broke your heart, I'll put it back together, I would wait forever.   13

And I heard it snap, it kind of sounded like you're never coming back.   17

About the Author   20

This empty canvas that they misunderstood, I wanna paint you in it but I'm not good.

The sound of our shoes as it tapped down on the floor was the only noise that could be heard in the building. It was almost six in the evening— the museum's about to close, but we only arrived a few minutes ago.

"We're kind of lucky that we got here at this hour, no?" I whispered as much as my breath could. My usual loud and noisy nature clashes with where I am, yet he would always say that I am the personification of a museum. He giggled softly as a response: "yeah, there's literally no one here except us and the guards."

We continued strolling around the area, trying to contain our excitement when we saw something cool or an eye-pleasing art. This has been our favorite hangout activity— visiting museums. We were not artistic per se, but something about looking at art and collections from the past makes us think that we were being brought back in time to where it all started. Like, like we could relate to it somehow.

This time, we visited the Yuchengco Museum in Makati city. It was, so far, the farthest museum that we have been to. It had four floors, yet we were only allowed to go up to the third.

Out of all the museums we've been to, this was my favorite one. Aside from the fact that we have the whole place to ourselves, it was small amongst all the places we've visited, but something about this place screams—us.

The second floor was dedicated to Rizal, the Philippine national hero; his life and works. He started reading statements from the wall about Rizal and I added information I learned in class. "Oh, did you know that Rizal was the first chess master in the Philippines?" I said. He turned to me with a surprised face and said, "Really? I did not know that. Tell me more."

"Yeah, he used to play with other Filipinos or foreigners he had met and socialized with, also with the guardia civiles; can you imagine that?" he shaked his head, indicating his disbelief. "I thought, mister Eugene Torre was Philippine's first chess master." I shrugged my shoulders in reply because I did not have an idea about the person that he mentioned.

At times like this, I am really grateful to myself for listening during our class discussions. "Look at that picture," I pointed at a frame, "chess pieces that he made." he squinted his eyes at the picture, like he was analyzing it. "He made that? Oh wow."

That is one thing I have loved about him. He always listens to me like every word that slips out of my tongue is a gem he treasures. I was sure that if anyone could hear our conversations, they would die out of boredom— but never once did he make me feel like that. I stared at him as he looked at the paintings in awe. My lips automatically formed a smile.

Suddenly, something in the background caught my attention. There was a different staircase leading down to the corner partition of the floor. It was a small exhibit that focused on Leonor Rivera, her life, and memorabilia. As far as I know, Leonor Rivera was one of the girls Rizal dated back then. But what made her so special that they had to put a focused corner for her in here? I was curious as hell.

The area down there could probably fit two to three people at a time, as it was too packed with remnants and relics. On the right side, there was an old furniture set and large picture frames hanging on the wall. There was a description that read, "*a loveseat in crewel featured in Leonor Rivera's home.*" on the left part stands a glass box that contains ancient clothing—*baro at saya*, which were the blouse and skirt that Leonor Rivera wore back then.

As I was walking down the stairs, I noticed a woman, around her late thirties or early forties, wearing a jet-black dress that reached above her knees. She had long, straight hair that went below her shoulders. She was standing still in front of a large frame, intently reading the words inscribed. I stood still at the end of the stairs so as not to disturb her or her space.

But my presence did not go unnoticed by her as she turned her head slowly to face me. Her eyes were fixated on me as fat tears rolled down her cheeks, and the way her eyes were colored bloodshot red implies that she had been crying for a long time. I wanted to utter a word to say something and ask, "*are you okay?*" but I could not. With the heavy air, the only sound that could pierce the silence was the soft, rhythmic cadence of her stifled sobs.

Before I could even react, we both heard footsteps above. "There you are," I heard him say. I turned to my back to see him walking down the stairs towards me. As if on cue, the woman rushed to walk up the stairs and went away.

Weird. That was hella weird.

He moved around the area and started scanning. I could hear him whisper "*wows*" and "*cool*" when he saw something that enticed him. Meanwhile, I was there—still standing at the end of the staircase, looking at Rivera's picture frame. As my feet dragged me in front of her sanctuary, got heavier and heavier with every step, like there was some kind of magnetic force.

Finally, I was able to read the inscription on the frame.

Leonor Rivera was born to a wealthy and influential family, as did Rizal. In 1880, Rizal and Rivera's paths met, and they got engaged within the same year. However, they kept their relationship a secret.

Rizal left the country for Europe as he became involved with the propaganda movement while still being in contact with his fiancé through letters. In 1887, Rizal published his novel, Noli Me Tangere, which immortalizes Rivera as Maria Clara.

With Rizal in a hot position with the church and Spanish government, Rivera's mother decided to interfere in the relationship with Rizal and her daughter by bribing the postman to give her the letters Rizal sent instead of Rivera. Rizal, on the other hand, was baffled after getting no response from his lover. He thought Rivera was angry at him.

After 10 years of being together, Rivera called it quits after having no contact with Rizal and complied with her mother's wishes about being engaged and married to Charles Henry Kipping, a British engineer.

However, in 1890, one of Rizal's letters was accidentally delivered to Rivera. She discovered that Rizal still loved her, and she confronted her mother about it. Defeated, her mother gave all of the unopened letters from Rizal over the years. But it was all too late. Rivera could not abort her engagement to kipping, whom she had already promised to marry.

"What the fuck," I breathed. "What the actual fuck," it was the only words I could utter as an empathetic pang reverberated through my heart. I winced, "Why is this so sad?"

"What is it? What is happening?" he popped out from my side suddenly. My eyes were still fixated on the frame and the words inscribed on it, like I was digesting every line of it. I released a hearty chuckle, trying to lessen the sadness I felt, "it is so sad, it hurts."

"They were meant to love each other, but not to be together," he said, which only made me sadder. "Well, fuck that. They should have been together," I retaliated.

He chuckled before pinching my cheek, "Sometimes, fate does that, and we could not do anything about it."

Yeah, fate could be a real jerk sometimes.

Why can't we for once say what we want, say what we feel.

It had been almost a decade of knowing each other, and it took me half of those years to come to the conclusion that I indeed, had feelings for him. Never once in those years did I attempt to say something about it or do something about it because I'm afraid. Don't we all? Imagine being with a person for almost the majority of your life, and suddenly, you were faced with a fifty-fifty situation where one wrong choice—you could lose it all. *Nope, I'm not risking it.* So instead, I bask in the comfort of being beside him even if the thought that we had not been together tortured me every single day.

Yet, I found it funny how knowing the tragic love story of Rizal and Rivera made me consider it— *confessing.* So, what if he does not reciprocate my feelings and only sees me as his little sister, and so what if he decides to cut me off because he gets uncomfortable? Then, okay... *okay, I'm not going to do it!*

The alarm sound of the train, indicating that the doors were about to close, burst my thought bubbles. I stared at our reflection on the window in front as the train moved swiftly. "You alright?" he asked. I nodded my head as a response. "Tired now, no?" his lips turned up in a knowing smile, which made me chuckle lightly. I nodded again, "yeah, my energy is so drained." suddenly, he tapped on his shoulders. "Come, close your eyes and rest for a bit," he signaled me to lean my head on his shoulders. I smiled and did so. Again, I stared at our reflection on the window in front as the train moved swiftly.

I loved this. I would not trade anything in this world for this. But should I settle for only this?

"Hey," I sat up straight and faced him. "I have something to tell you." *Miss Leonor Rivera, please give me all the strength and courage to tell him everything. Please. Please. Please.*

He nodded his head and signaled me to go on. "So, we had been friends for a long time now, and I just wanted to say that—" I was cut off by his phone ringing. He quickly fished out his phone from his pocket and looked at me apologetically. I signaled him to take the call first, smiling.

Was that your sign to not do it, Miss Leonor?

Amidst the noise of the train as it passed on the tracks and the silent murmurs of the people on board, there was one sound that stood out above all—the delicate symphony of his giggles. It was not just any type of laughter; it was a melody that resonated deep within my heart. He sounded very happy with the person he was talking to on the phone. Maybe that was enough reason.

He lowered his phone, and a smile lingers on his face. "What was that again?"

"Nothing," I smiled. "I am just thankful that all these years have passed and you are still here."

Yeah, i should not risk all of these.

Call in the morning, say that you love me, I'm always waiting, I'm always waiting.

That was three years ago. Everything has changed now.

Our friendship had an unspoken pact, an unwavering bond that has weathered the storms of being an adolescent to the highs and lows of entering adulthood. But as we entered new chapters of our lives, the red string of fate began to pull us in different directions—slowly and gradually—that we both did not see it coming until it did.

Oh, I still think about him day by day. How were his dogs? Do they still jump on him as soon as he enters the house? How were his job applications? Did he cry like I did when I got rejected on my first interview? How were his mother and his sister? Do they still ask him how I have been? And how is he doing now? Are you alright with where you are right now?

Oh, and I still think about that day. What could happen if I said it right there and then. Will our fate be different to what we have right now?

That was my train of thought as I stare at my phone, vibrating with his name plastered. As the phone rings,

I could feel the rush of memories flooding my mind— like I am being transported to a different time and place. Like I am still with him, and the last three years did not happen.

With my shaky hands, I managed to click on the green icon. There is a pause and a breath before I heard a sound, "hello?"

Of course, I am surged with surprise, and a moment of disbelief as I try to reconcile the voice on the other side of the phone with the person that I have memories with. The anticipation builds up, my heart racing, and my palms sweats— "hi," I replied.

"Oh gosh, how are you? How have you been?" like the uncertainty I had before were not enough, another series of unanswered questions quickly piled up my mind: what is happening? Why is he calling me now? Why did it take three years? What does he want?

"Is it okay for us to meet?"

Miss leonor, is this you telling me that now is the right time?

"Sure."

I promise you, Miss Leonor, this is the last time.

Broke your heart, I'll put it back together, I would wait forever.

I am sitting down, feeling giddy with butterflies bursting on my stomach. I am wearing a dress, my favorite type of clothing. The fabric, a delicate yet elegant jet-black color—his favorite, clung to my figure with a grace that accentuated my curves.

It was the sound of the bell as the door opened that made me sit up straight. I immediately saw him entering, and the first thought that went through my mind is "he changed."

"Hi," he says as his feet drag him towards the booth I am sitting in. Hearing his voice succumbs me to a nostalgia that envelops me like a warm blanket in my hometown, bringing the fragments of our shared memories. The hours of catching up with him feels like a bittersweet embrace of the past, reminding me of the person we used to be and the connections that we once made in our lives. It creates a vivid tapestry of emotions, tugging on the red string of my heart.

This is it, Miss Leonor.

"I have something to tell you," I started, but before I could even continue, his phone rings. Immediately, he excused himself and went outside the café. The frustration manifested as a tight knot on my chest, a tension that I always refused to dissipate. Everything is a maddening dance with repetition, the same issues of being afraid of confessing and trying to, only to be cut off. It feels like the wheels of my time had been stuck in a timeless loop, replaying the same scenes of disappointment and unanswered questions.

The more that I tried to break free from this loop, the more it seemed to tighten its grip on me.

On the moment he got back to the booth, his face displayed the same smile I saw three years ago. It is a moment I have always filled with joy and excitement, but now— with reflection and introspection. *Is all of these worth the heartbreak?*

"So, the reason I called you," he started, "I am getting married."

I felt the earth fell into a heavy silence, only to be shattered by the lingering echoes of his words that was dropped like a bomb. The wheels of my time that I suspected as a loop seemed like it freezes for a moment, until I felt it break into pieces that slowly and gradually pierced through my heart until it numbed.

I took a breath, and another one. "Really?" I uttered, forcing a smile. His face chimed brightly, something I have never seen before. "Yeah, actually it is a long story."

"I remember seeing you back in fourth grade and having this massive crush on you, because why not? You are not hard to like," while he is composed and collected as he declares what he had felt before, I was sitting there—trying to hold it all together before my tear ducts betray me and burst. "I never thought that we would be friends, best of friends— that massive crush I had on you turned into something more and deep. To be frank, I loved you so much."

Loved. He *loved* me.

"Back then, I contemplated a lot of times on whether I should confess to you or not because I do not want to put our friendship at risk. I was so afraid to lose you that I pushed out the thought of having you mine."

Afraid. He was *afraid.*

"You were out of my league, like they have always said to me. You are you, and i am just me. So, instead of telling you directly—I wrote you letters over the years to cope and to express my feelings towards you until I have nothing left to write."

Letters. He wrote me *letters.*

"When we started to drift apart, that was when I met her. I could say that she is my Kairos, something that happened to me unexpectedly that turned my life in a new perspective. She is great, she is my strength, and she has given me the courage to power through every day since I have met her, and I love her so much. But you know—sometimes, I think about what could have happened if I told you that I loved you?"

He released a hearty chuckle, continuing,"nonetheless, everything turned out great for us. I cannot afford to lose you. We are great off as friends, right?"

The initial pang on my heart as it breaks was expected but followed that was a snap. The once bittersweet melody of our past echoing through the chambers of my heart, turned into pieces of melancholic refrain of separation. But amidst the swirling emotions, there was a quiet acceptance that settled within me. With all the strength I could muster, I pushed up the corners of my lips.

"I could not agree more."

And I heard it snap, it kind of sounded like you're never coming back.

The aftermath of everything becomes a heavy fog that settles over my emotions. The world around me continues to revolve at its normal pace, and I feel like a spectator, observing life through a haze. Unconsciously, my feet drag me to the place where it all began—where we began. In the heart of Makati City, to the very place that witnessed it all.

The murmuring conversations feel like distant echoes, and the canvases are merely blurred pages. People are scattered all over the museum, yet all I could hear was the heaviness of my feet as they trampled down on the floor. The eyes that used to wander around to savor the aesthetics of my favorite place—now a navigator through the foggy landscape of numbness.

Here I am, once again looking at you, Miss Leonor.

Here I am, once again reading the words inscribed on your frame, letting every letter sink in.

I want to cry. I want to cry it all out.

Miss Leonor, what did you do when you found out that Rizal still loved you? Did you weep? Did you cry? Were you angry at him, or were you angry at yourself? Did you regret not saying anything to him? Did you regret not saying anything at all? Did you blame yourself when you found out?

Because I cannot control my tears now that they have started to fall. My weak sobs are for your ears to hear. I am angry at him for not saying anything, but I am more enraged at myself for letting the years fly by without doing anything. I deeply regret that I said everything, but exactly those three words could have saved everything. And now, I blame myself that it all turned out like this when I had fate dancing in my palms the whole time.

The feeling of being hurt for another person is not a normal bodily sensation; it is a simultaneous throb of physical wounds and the intangible bonds of empathy within us that intertwine our lives through the acts of bravery, love, and the enduring echoes of choices that we have made for the sake of another person.

The first time I found out Rivera's story, I was engulfed with heartache and sadness for her situation, not knowing that I would go through the same thing she did. Maybe, so did the woman I saw before. After all, all the hurt and sadness that we have felt are the consequences of our intertwined lives. And the choices that we have made for the sake of another person are to blame for the endless loop of time in our lives.

The creaking sound of the staircase snapped me out of my wandering thoughts. Quickly, my head whips to the other side—and there was a girl staring at me with bewilderment. Probably wondering why I was crying my heart out in front of a picture frame like a mad woman.

I turned my body to face her and started walking towards her. My eyes are like broken faucets, as they continue to let out more tears with every step that I take.

I took a long breath and said, "do it."

"Tell them everything before it gets too late. Tell them that you love them, that you care for them, that they make you happy. Tell them that they are what your dreams are about, that you always talk about them to your friends. Tell them how much your heart aches for them and how your heart wishes to be with them. Tell them what you feel before you choke with all the words that got stuck in your throat over the years, and now you are crying it all out. Say something, please."

About the Author

Densei

The creative mind behind the words, Densei, is a passionate storyteller that is currently navigating through life of being college student.

As a Psychology major at Far Eastern University in the Philippines, Densei dives into an adventure to her literary pursuits—providing a unique lens on how she views the world.

Beyond the academic realm, she is also an active member of their institute's official publication specifically in the literary department, where she contributes and hones her craft to the vibrant literary culture in their campus.

Despite literature not being her major, reading and writing had always been Densei's comfort. Aside from being a counselor, her greatest dream is to write a piece that could make someone feel seen and heard.

www.ingramcontent.com/pod-product-compliance
Lightning Source LLC
LaVergne TN
LVHW041602070526
838199LV00046B/2107